To my daughter, Kellie:
Remember there is nothing you can't achieve
if you have courage and faith.
— J. C.

For my children, Jack, Sam, Catherine, and Anna
— J. W.

Introduction

We Both Read books can be read alone or with another person. If you are reading the book alone, you can read it like any other book. If you are reading with another person, you can take turns reading aloud. If you are taking turns, the reader with more experience should read the parts marked with a red star ★. The reader with less experience should read the parts marked with a blue star ★. As you read, you will notice some difficult words introduced in sections with a red star, then repeated in sections with a blue star. You can recognize these words by their **bold lettering**.

Sharing the reading of a book can be a lot of fun, and reading aloud is a great way to improve fluency and expression. If you are reading with someone else, you might also want to take the time, while reading the book, to interact and talk about what is happening in the story. After reading with someone else, you might even want to experience reading the entire book on your own.

The Boy Who Carried the Flag

We Both Read® Chapter Book

HISTORICAL FICTION

Text Copyright © 2010 by Jana Carson
Illustrations Copyright © 2010 by Johanna Westerman
All rights reserved

We Both Read® is a trademark of Treasure Bay, Inc.

Published by
Treasure Bay, Inc.
P. O. Box 119
Novato, CA 94948 USA

Printed in Singapore

Library of Congress Catalog Card Number: 2010921690

Hardcover ISBN-13: 978-1-60115-247-3
Paperback ISBN-13: 978-1-60115-248-0

We Both Read® Books
Patent No. 5,957,693

Visit us online at:
www.webothread.com

PR 11-14

WE BOTH READ®

The Boy Who Carried the Flag

BY JANA CARSON

ILLUSTRATED BY JOHANNA WESTERMAN

CONTENTS

TREASURE BAY

CHAPTER 1

Sun Up to Sun Down

★ "Run! Run!!" I heard a voice inside my head screaming. I knew I was dreaming, but I couldn't wake up. I'd had this frightening dream before. It was always the same. I was all alone and it was very cold. I knew I should run, but I was too frightened to move.

"Get up, Ben!" yelled my little sister, Grace. I sat up quickly, my heart still pounding from my dream. "Ma's got your breakfast in a pail, and Pa is waiting for you in the field."

It didn't take long for me to figure out that I had overslept.

★　　I jumped into my clothes and flew down the ladder from the loft. I missed a step and almost fell on the way down.

"I'm sorry I woke up late, Ma," I said, grabbing the pail as I ran for the door.

"If you're not truly sorry now, you will be when your Pa gets a hold of you," she called after me.

I raced from the farmhouse to meet Pa in the field. I could see the sun just beginning to climb up into the sky.

★ Our farmhouse sat in the valley next to the great White Mountains. Pa thought it was the most beautiful spot in the whole colony of New Hampshire, but living on the farm was hard. We worked from sun up to sun down. Ma cooked, cleaned, and washed our clothes. Grace fed the chickens and helped Ma with the cleaning. I milked the cow and helped Pa with the crops.

Pa was already tending the field when I came rushing towards him. "You're late," he scolded. Then he looked me in the eyes and quietly added, "These are **troubled** times, Ben, and a boy your age ought to know what's expected of him."

Pa was right. I wasn't a baby anymore. There was talk of war all through the American colonies, and some boys not much older than me had already joined the army.

Without saying another word, Pa pointed to the horse. It was time to hitch up the plow and get to work.

★ "I'm sorry I was late again, Pa," I said, not looking at him. "I've really let you down."

"You could never let me down," Pa said with a wink. Then he headed for the barn and I got to work.

Working alone in the field gave me time to think. I thought about my bad dreams and what Pa had said about the **troubled** times. I didn't know yet just how much my life was about to change.

CHAPTER 2

Troubled Times

★ "There's going to be a town meeting!" I hollered to Pa from across the yard as I hurried toward the barn to show him the notice. Pa took a quick look at it and said, "Hitch up the wagon, Ben."

"Can I go too, Pa?" I asked. He thought about it for a few seconds and then nodded his head.

The town meeting was being held in a place called Hanover. It was a small town with a few lumber mills, a general store, and a big church right in the center. As we rode in, I saw a large group of men marching in the street with guns. "Are those men in the army, Pa?" I asked.

"No, son. Those men are part of the **militia**. A militia is a group of ordinary working men like me who get together in times of trouble to protect the town."

"Is there going to be trouble, Pa?"

"I hope not," he answered with a worried look on his face.

★ The meeting was held at the church. Many seats were filled with **militia** men who had come from other towns far away. Some of the men were shouting, and they seemed angry. A tall man stood up and walked to the front of the church. He held up his hands to quiet the crowd.

"The King of England is making us pay high taxes," he said in a booming voice. "The King believes that our homes and our lives belong to him. I believe that we are Americans and our lives belong to us!" The men all cheered as he added, "It is time for all of us to stand up and fight!"

★ It was just turning dark when we finally got back home from the town meeting. I was very tired as I climbed up the ladder to the loft and crawled into my bed. Just as I was about to close my eyes, I heard a loud knock on the door.

"Who could be calling at this time of night?" I heard Ma ask.

Curious, I crawled to the edge of the loft and peeked down. I saw several big men standing on our porch. The man in front of the group was Ethan Allen, the man who had led the town meeting. I wondered what he was doing here. My heart sank when I heard his words:

"A small group of **British soldiers** are camped at Fort Ticonderoga. If we act now, we can stage a surprise attack and capture the fort."

★ The men sat around the table speaking in hushed voices for a long time. They wanted Pa to lead them along the secret Indian hunting trails in the mountains. That way they could take the **British soldiers** by surprise. Pa was nodding his head. He seemed ready to do what they asked. I was scared. I didn't want Pa to get hurt.

★ I awoke early the next morning with a sick feeling in my stomach. I knew it was wrong, but I felt angry at Pa. How could he risk his life to go off and lead those men in a surprise attack?

I dressed quickly and climbed down the ladder. Ma was sitting by the fire in her rocking chair. "Your Pa is gone," she said softly.

"I know. I heard the men talking last night," I answered. "Why did Pa do it?"

"He believes that what he is doing is right, Ben. He has gone to help fight for our freedom."

From that point on, time seemed to fly. Every day there was more news of fights breaking out between the British soldiers and the American militia. We prayed each night for Pa to come home safely.

CHAPTER 3

Unexpected Kindness

★ Several weeks later, I was out working in the field when I spotted something in the distance. Some men were marching down the path toward our farm. I knew they were British soldiers by the bright red coats they were wearing. I ran as fast as I could back to the house.

Ma was standing on the front porch. She had seen the soldiers too. "Should I get my hunting gun?" I asked, out of breath from running.

"No! I don't want any shooting." Ma tried to sound calm as she added, "They are men, Ben, not squirrels."

"Then what should I do?" I cried.

"Hide!" she answered quickly.

"Let me stay with you," I begged.

"Take your sister and run for the barn," Ma insisted. "GO!" I quickly grabbed Grace's hand and we ran.

When we got to the barn, I helped Grace find a hiding place in the hay loft.

"You stay here, Grace," I instructed my sister. "I'm going back to the house to help Ma. Those soldiers have no right to be here. It's our farm!"

Just then, I understood why Pa had left us to go and fight. He was right. Our freedom was worth fighting for.

★ I ran back toward the barn door. Suddenly, I felt two big hands grab me from behind. I was lifted high into the air and thrown over someone's shoulder like a sack of potatoes. I was being carried by a big man wearing hawk feathers braided into his long, black hair. I saw a smaller man beside him. Indians!

I struggled to get free from my enemies, but the Indian who carried me held on tight.

★   "Let me go!" I yelped. And, to my surprise, the Indian gently placed me on the ground.

"We will not hurt you," he said. "There are others here from my tribe who are watching out for your mother. I promise you that she will not be harmed."

"Why are the soldiers here?" I asked.

"They are searching the house for your father," he answered. "He has asked us to come and take your family away from this place."

"Pa sent you?" I asked in **disbelief**.

"Yes," he continued. "You are no longer safe here. Your father wants us to take you to your uncle's house in **Philadelphia**."

I realized now that these were my pa's friends. Their names were Keeper and Spirit. It was Keeper who had taught my pa about the secret trails in the White Mountains.

★   We left the farm that night and headed for the city of **Philadelphia**. I could tell that Ma had been crying. She tried to put on a cheerful face as she told me, "You're going to love the city."

My sister Grace looked at Ma with **disbelief** and cried, "I'm going to hate it!"

No one spoke after that. All I could hear was the steady clip clop of the horses' feet as they pulled the heavy wagon. Pa had always said, "Never judge a book by its cover." These Indians turned out to be our friends, not our enemies. I felt safe with them riding beside our wagon.

★   We were exhausted from the long journey as our wagon pulled up to the big house in Philadelphia. My Uncle Will threw open the door and came to the wagon with open arms. "Your beds are all ready," he said kindly. "Come inside now. We'll unload the wagon in the morning."

I followed Uncle Will up a winding staircase to the top floor. He led me to a room that had the biggest feather bed in it that I had ever seen. I crawled into bed and quickly drifted off to sleep.

I was still dreaming when I felt the bed shake. "Wake up, sleepy head!" my sister Grace chirped, giving the bed one final shake. "We're having breakfast in the dining room!"

I got dressed quickly and rushed downstairs.

★   The late morning sun was shining brightly through the windows of the dining room. Everyone was seated around the table in fancy chairs.

"I'm sorry I'm late for breakfast," I said politely.

Ma smiled at me and proudly announced, "Uncle Will has found both of us a job, Ben!"

I must have looked very surprised because Ma went on to say, "Times are hard and everyone has to pitch in, Son. We'll be working for a nice lady in town named Betsy Ross. We start tomorrow."

⭐   I was so excited about my new job that I could hardly sleep that night. The sun was just coming up when I got out of bed the next morning. I could hear Uncle Will outside, hitching the horse to the wagon.

After breakfast, we headed out. As we rode through town, I noticed that many of the houses in Philadelphia were big and fancy like my uncle's house. There were all sorts of shops along the main street. We stopped in front of a nice house with a sign in front that read: "Fine **Upholstery** Work Done Here."

We were greeted at the front door by a pleasant lady. "My name is Betsy Ross," she said. "Welcome to Philadelphia."

18

CHAPTER 4

A True Patriot

★ Working at the **upholstery** shop kept Ma and me very busy. I kept the fires going in all of the fireplaces and made deliveries around the city. Ma helped Mrs. Ross with the cutting and sewing. It had been three weeks since we left our farm to come to Philadelphia. We hadn't heard from Pa, but I hoped that he was safe.

"We need more firewood in the parlor, Ben," Mrs. Ross said, pulling me away from my thoughts. I nodded and headed outside.

I noticed a crisp chill in the air as I made my way to the woodpile. Winter was on its way. I filled the box with firewood and bent down to pick up the heavy load.

"Ben, come quickly!" I heard Ma's voice shout excitedly.

Ma met me halfway as I ran toward the house. "What is it?" I asked, slightly out of breath.

"We have news about Pa," she answered joyfully.

★ I let out a great shout. "Where is he? Is he safe? Did they capture Fort **Ticonderoga**?"

"Let's get inside before we freeze to death," Ma said, smiling. "There is someone here who can answer all of your questions."

Betsy Ross was standing next to a very tall gentleman in the parlor. I knew right away that he must be someone important. "Ben, I'd like you to meet General George Washington," she said proudly.

I had never met such a famous person before. General Washington was a **patriot** and the leader of the American **Continental Army**. Stories about him appeared in every newspaper.

★ "How do you do, sir?" I said as General Washington bent down to shake my hand.

"It has come to my attention that it was your father who led the Green Mountain Boys to Fort **Ticonderoga**," he said in a strong, clear voice.

"Yes, sir," I answered respectfully. "Is Pa all right?"

"Your father is alive and well," General Washington answered. "The fort was captured without anyone getting hurt. Your father and the other men were able to take much needed supplies from the fort. They walked many miles to bring those supplies to me and the **Continental Army**." Then he looked me in the eyes and added, "Your father is a hero and a true **patriot**."

My heart filled with pride. "Thank you, sir."

★ General Washington told me that Pa had joined the army and was now fighting with a small troop of men near Canada. I wished I could be there to fight with him. He then showed me a piece of paper with a hand-drawn picture of a flag on it.

"What's this?" I asked.

"I hope this will be the new flag that brings all of the American colonies together," he answered. "Right now, the soldiers need one flag to remind them that it takes courage and strength to build a nation." He handed the picture of the flag to Betsy Ross.

"I'll give this my full effort, General Washington," she promised. He thanked her, then slipped quietly out the backdoor.

★ It had been several weeks since General Washington's visit. The news about the war had not been good lately. The papers said General George Washington had lost a lot of battles. It looked like we might lose the war. I felt that the flag was needed more than ever now.

It was the week of Christmas when we saw British soldiers marching through the streets as we made our way to the shop. I looked at Ma with great concern. I wondered if Betsy Ross was ever going to complete the flag for General Washington.

When we arrived at the shop that morning, Betsy Ross was standing in the middle of the room. She was proudly holding up the finished flag.

"How do you like it?" she asked.

"It's beautiful," I replied.

CHAPTER 5

Alone in the Dark

★   I knew when I saw the flag that it would bring hope and courage to General Washington and his men.

Betsy Ross started to speak. "I wish there was a way . . ." She didn't finish her sentence. Her voice choked up and her eyes filled with tears. I knew what she wanted to say.

"There has to be a way to get this flag to the General and his men," I said firmly. Then I said something that surprised even me. "Let me take it to them."

"Ben! No!" Ma cried out.

"There are plenty of boys my age fighting in the war," I protested. "Please let me do this, Ma!"

"We don't even know where General Washington is," Ma declared. "The papers say that his troops are on the run and the British are chasing close behind."

"I might know where he is," Betsy Ross said. Ma and I looked at her in amazement. "I heard some **confidential information** last night. If it's true, there may still be some hope of our winning this war."

★   "What **confidential information**?" Ma and I asked at the same time.

"I heard from a good source that General Washington has secretly moved his troops nearby," Betsy Ross said in a hushed voice. "He's planning a surprise attack on the British soldiers who have taken over the town of Trenton."

★ "Even if that's true, I can't let Ben deliver the flag," Ma said. "It's too dangerous. And it's almost Christmas!"

"Please, Ma," I pleaded. "I have to try. Let me do this . . . for Pa and for all the men who are fighting for our freedom."

Ma sighed. Her face was sad, but also proud, as she finally agreed to let me go.

We all sat down and made a plan. There was no time to lose. The information was that General Washington's troops were secretly camped out near the bank of the **Delaware River** across from Trenton. They would cross the Delaware River on Christmas night and take their enemy by surprise the next day.

Our plan was that Uncle Will would take me as far as he could by wagon. From there I'd have to find the way by myself. I wasn't afraid. Pa had taught me how to read signs along the trails and how to survive in bad weather. "There are British soldiers everywhere," Uncle Will warned. "You'll have to hide in the back of the wagon."

★ We left late that afternoon. Betsy Ross gave me the flag in a leather pouch and Ma handed me a small pack of food and supplies. I climbed into the back of Uncle Will's wagon, and Ma covered me with old blankets.

"Good luck, Son," Ma whispered.

As we rode out of town, the temperature began to drop, and the wind was starting to blow in from the north. The road was bumpy, and my body felt sore from being thrown around. After what seemed like a long time, the wagon finally stopped.

"This is as far as I can take you," Uncle Will said as he lifted the blankets. The wind was blowing hard, and it was beginning to snow. "Make your way through the trees until you come to a clearing in the woods. Walk in the same direction until you reach the bank of the **Delaware River**," he said. "I'll come back to look for you in three days. There's enough food and supplies in your pack to last until then." I could tell that Uncle Will didn't want to leave me.

"Don't worry about me, Uncle Will," I said. "I'll find my way."

★ I watched the light of the **lantern** on Uncle Will's wagon until it disappeared.

The wind picked up, and the snow was falling heavily now. I held up my lantern, hoping to see my way through the blinding snow. Whoosh! A blast of cold air hit me with a force so strong that it knocked me off my feet. I watched in horror as the light in my lantern flickered and the flame went out. The light was getting dim and the snow was falling in thick, white sheets all around me. I could barely see my hands in front of my face. I felt a wave of panic and fear sweep over me. I forced myself to start walking. I stumbled over rocks and felt tree branches scratching the skin on my face. Finally, my eyes began to adjust to the dimming light and falling snow, and I saw a clearing up ahead.

★ I followed the clearing to the bank of the river. I had made it this far, but I didn't know what to do next. Then I heard a big splashing noise out on the water. I strained my eyes to try and see what had made the sound. I looked at the **lantern** hanging uselessly in my hand. If only I had some light! I heard the noise again, only this time it sounded closer.

Suddenly, it became clear what had made the noise. It was a boat, and it was heading for the shore. I froze in my tracks.

It was just like my dream. I was all alone. It was very cold, and I was too frightened to move. I held on tightly to the leather case with the flag in it. "I must have courage," I thought. "People are counting on me."

CHAPTER 6

Muskets and Rifles

★ The men in the boat were speaking in a language that I didn't understand. Gathering my nerve, I moved a branch out of the way to get a better look.

SNAP!

The sound of the branch breaking seemed loud enough to be heard for miles. I held my breath and tried not to move or make a sound. Slowly turning, I peeked through the branches again. They were gone! The boat was there, but the men had **vanished**.

Then the cold hard steel of a knife point touched the back of my neck. I shut my eyes and prepared for the worst.

"Please don't kill me," I begged.

"Ben? Is that you?" the man asked in perfect English. It was Keeper and his son Spirit!

★ "What are you doing out here all alone?" Keeper asked. I was so happy I wanted to shout for joy at the sight of them. "Come," Keeper said, "You look like you could use a hot meal." All of my fear **vanished**, and I was suddenly aware of how hungry I was.

That night, as we sat by the fire, I told Keeper and Spirit about the flag and how important it was that I get it to General Washington. I knew that if Pa had trusted them to get us to Philadelphia, I could trust them now. They listened quietly as I explained everything.

"Do you know where General Washington and his troops might be camped?" I asked, hoping that they might have seen something.

★ "We passed many boats hidden along the shore not far from here," Spirit said.

My heart jumped at this news.

"You must sleep now," Keeper said softly. "We will leave when the sun comes up in the morning."

In no time, Keeper and Spirit put up a shelter facing away from the cold wind that was blowing off the river. I still held the flag as I drifted off to sleep under the warm bearskin blankets inside the shelter.

It was dawn when Keeper woke me up. The temperature had dropped, and it was getting colder by the minute.

Indians call their boats **canoes**. Keeper's canoe was filled with animal furs and fresh fish that had frozen during the night. No one spoke as the canoe slipped over the water.

Suddenly I realized that it was Christmas morning. "Ma must be sick with worry," I shouted abruptly.

"Shhh," Keeper hissed. "The shore of this river hides many enemies."

I remained silent for the rest of the journey.

★ We traveled for a long time. Finally, Keeper pointed to a patch of bushes. He steered the **canoe** to the shore. Spirit jumped into the icy river. Then he pulled the canoe behind a bush. "We will wait here," Keeper said.

I saw lots of other boats hidden in the bushes. They had to be the boats General Washington and his troops would use to cross the river. We had to be in the right place.

★ We waited for several hours until Keeper finally said, "We must leave now. It is too cold for us to stay."

"No!" I cried, trying hard to control my emotions. "Don't you understand? I have to give this flag to General Washington. It's a flag of courage and strength!"

Just then, I thought I heard something. "What's that?" I whispered, standing up to get a look. It was faint at first, but now I clearly heard the sound of men marching.

"Stay down!" Keeper said, pulling me back down in the canoe. "It may be your enemies." They were so close now that I could hear the men's voices.

"They're Americans!" I whispered, as I peeked through the reeds at the troops gathering on the river bank. Some of the men carried **rifles**, while others were holding **muskets** over their shoulders.

★ The men looked very tired. Some of them had nothing on their feet but rags. Others had no coats. Still they marched with their heads held up high.

I saw a man on a tall horse trotting up through the line of soldiers. "General Washington," I called out before Keeper could stop me.

Click! Click! Click!

Every man with a **rifle** or **musket** turned and aimed his gun right at me.

CHAPTER 7

Hope and Courage

★ "Hold your fire!" General Washington ordered the men.

I scrambled from the boat and made my way to the shore. The tears were freezing on my face as I ran forward through the confused soldiers toward General Washington. "What are you doing here, boy?" he asked, getting down from his horse.

"I have something to give to you, sir." I answered.

My hands were shaking from the cold as I carefully opened the leather pouch and presented the flag to General Washington. "You told me that it would help remind the men to have courage and strength," I said, trying to steady my voice. "I...I thought the men might need it tonight."

General Washington stood silent for a moment. "I am overcome and humbled by your actions," he said quietly.

★   Then he gave an order for all of the troops to gather around. He mounted his horse and held the flag up high for the men to see.

"This boy risked his life on Christmas Day to bring us this flag of liberty! Are we ready to risk our lives for freedom?" General Washington asked his men.

The men raised their arms and cheered in agreement.

"Sir," I said, feeling small next to the giant horse. "May I carry the flag into battle?"

"You have done enough," he answered.

But I wasn't going to take no for an answer. "Please, sir. I want to fight for my country—like my pa."

George Washington looked at me with understanding. "All right," he said finally. "I'll put you between two of my best men."

★ We had to win this battle or the war might be lost. George Washington knew that the enemy soldiers who had taken over the town of **Trenton** would not be expecting an attack on the day after Christmas.

The storm was so fierce that our boats barely made it across the Delaware River through the howling wind and heavy snow. As soon as we pulled the boats on shore, General Washington sent troops moving quickly in all directions so the enemy soldiers could not escape.

"Don't let any harm come to this boy," General Washington said to several soldiers who were standing at attention.

Keeper and Spirit arrived behind us in their canoe, which was now also filled with soldiers.

BOOM! The sound of the cannon made the ground shake. The battle was on. All around me I could hear shouts and cries from the men and the ear-splitting sound of gunfire.

★ I held the flag up on its post as the battle of **Trenton** raged around me. Out of nowhere, an enemy soldier appeared. He charged toward me. "I'll never let him take down the flag," I thought. Two of our men tried to jump in his path, but he was too fast for them.

All of a sudden I heard a whizzing sound as one of our men fired a shot at the man running toward me. The man lifted his gun and fired back. I felt a white, hot pain in my right arm. I had been shot. The pain was terrible. My legs gave out, and I sank to my knees. I rested the flagpole against my chest, and I held on tightly with my left arm.

"No!" I heard Keeper scream as he came running toward me. Three other soldiers were running to help me as well. The last thing I saw was the beautiful flag waving proudly above me.

★ I woke up to the delicious aroma of Ma's biscuits baking in the kitchen hearth. I thought I must be dreaming. I opened my eyes wider to adjust to the brightness of the room.

"How are you feeling, Son?" Ma asked as she kissed me on the forehead. I couldn't believe it! I was alive, and I was back at home with my family.

"What happened?" I asked, feeling very confused.

"You carried the flag in a battle that will surely go down in history as the one that turned the tide for America," Uncle Will said proudly.

My spirits soared at this news. George Washington had done it. We had won the battle of Trenton. "How did I get here?" I asked.

"Keeper and Spirit brought you right to our door," my sister Grace eagerly told me. "You were in bad shape. The doctor didn't know if you were going to make it!"

Then Ma showed me a small box. "I'm sure General Washington would have liked to have given this to you himself," she said as she placed the box in my hands.

I opened the box quickly. "It's a button!" I said with surprise.

Ma nodded. "From General Washington's coat."

"You mean the coat that he wore in the battle?" I asked, amazed.

"That's right. And I have another surprise for you," Ma said as she handed me a letter.

"It's from Pa!" I shouted. I read the letter out loud.

"Son, your bravery gave hope to us all. The dream of what America can be shines brightly in your heart. I am so very proud of you. I'll be home soon. Love, Pa."

When I finished the letter, I folded it up and put it in the small box with the button. I held the box tightly, thinking of the two things held inside. I knew I would keep them both for the rest of my life.

If you liked *The Boy Who Carried the Flag*, here is another
We Both Read® book you are sure to enjoy!

The Mystery of Pirate's Point

The race is on! It's the annual swimming competition
and it looks like the boys' team is going to lose to the
girls' team again! The boys think some girls stole
their mascot named Lucky. Without their mascot,
the boys are convinced they will never win. Now
it's up to Sam and his friends to solve the mystery.
If they can find Lucky, maybe they can also solve
the old mystery of Pirate's Point!

To see all the We Both Read books that are available,
just go online to **www.webothread.com.**